THE PLANT RESCUER

MATTHEW RIVERA

NEAL PORTER BOOKS

HOLIDAY HOUSE / NEW YORK

Manny and his dad come from a long line of gardeners.

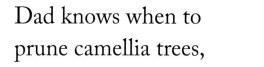Dad knows when to
prune camellia trees,

how to grow blue hydrangeas,

and which
plants attract
bees.

Manny wishes the apartment he and Dad share with Nana had a yard with flowers and trees.

CASA MARIPOSA

201

202

101

102

But Dad has a gift
for growing jungles in
the smallest spaces.

Manny loves visiting garden centers with his dad.

One day, he asks for a
plant of his very own.

"This plant belongs to you, muchacho. Take care of it and give it a good life."

"Don't worry, Dad! My amigo is in good hands."

Manny has never cared for
his own plant before.

Excitement leads to disappointment.

Manny thinks of ideas

to bring his amigo

back to life.

Nothing works.

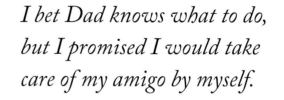

I bet Dad knows what to do, but I promised I would take care of my amigo by myself.

I have stacks of books about animals, dinosaurs, and even bugs, but nothing about plants.

A new day brings fresh ideas.

Indoor Plants

THE HOUSE Plant

Gardening

GARDEN PLANET

the GREAT LEAF

HOUSEPLANT GUIDE

GROW

INDOOR NATURE

Manny turns to his old friend, the library, for help.

He discovers the best spot for sunlight,

how much to water,

and when to snap off leaves to allow his plant to grow big and tall.

He learns about mulch and
how to make his own blend.

Singing is Manny's
extra touch.

His amigo grows,

and grows,

and GROWS.

"Manny! Look at your room! It's beautiful."

Manny's Room

"Mijo, let's share your gift and take cuttings of your amigo to our neighbors."

Manny is the youngest gardener
in a long line of gardeners.

For Mom and Dad: thank you
for always giving me enough space to grow.
For Gary: your love and support mean the world to me.

Neal Porter Books

HOLIDAY HOUSE is registered in the U.S. Patent and Trademark Office.

Printed and bound in January 2024 at Toppan Leefung, Dongguan City, China.

The artwork for this book was created with watercolors, acrylics, and digital tools.

Book design by Jennifer Browne

www.holidayhouse.com

First Edition

1 3 5 7 9 10 8 6 4 2

Library of Congress Cataloging-in-Publication Data

Names: Rivera, Matthew (Children's books illustrator), author, illustrator.

Title: The plant rescuer / Matthew Rivera.

Description: First. | New York : Neal Porter Books / Holiday House, 2024. |

Audience: Ages 4–8 | Audience: Grades K–1 | Summary: "A young boy learns
to care for his own plant, proudly taking after his gardener father."—
Provided by publisher.

Identifiers: LCCN 2023017080 | ISBN 9780823454990 (hardcover)

Subjects: CYAC: Gardening—Fiction. | Fathers and sons—Fiction. |
Perseverance—Fiction. | LCGFT: Picture books.

Classification: LCC PZ7.1.R5767 Pl 2024 | DDC [E]—dc23

LC record available at https://lccn.loc.gov/2023017080

ISBN: 978-0-8234-5499-0